GHOST IN THE HOUSE

HOUSE

Ammi-Joan Paquette

illustrated by
Adam Record

SCHOLASTIC INC.

BOO!

There's a ghost in the house,
In the creepy haunted house,
On this dark, spooky night, all alone.

And he goes slip-slide
With a swoop and a glide
Until suddenly he hears . . .

A GROAN!

And a mummy makes two in the house,
In the creepy haunted house,
On this dark, spooky night, on the prowl.

And they shuffle around
Without even a sound
Until suddenly they hear . . .

A GROWL!

And a monster makes three in the house,
In the creepy haunted house,
On this dark, spooky night, midnight black.

And they creep and crawl
Down the echoing hall
Until suddenly they hear . . .

CLICK-
CLACK!

And a skeleton makes four in the house,
In the creepy haunted house,
On this dark, spooky night, cold and bleak.

And they stagger and stomp
In a spine-chilling romp
Until suddenly they hear . . .

A SHRIEK!

And a witch makes five in the house,
In the creepy haunted house,
On this dark, spooky night — best beware!

Then a sudden FLASH
Makes them topple and crash,
And suddenly they hear . . .

"WHO'S THERE?"

There's a boy in the house,

In the creepy haunted house,

On this dark, spooky night — what a fright!

Five, four, three, two, one —
All the creatures run!
Leaving him alone to say . . .

"GOOD NIGHT!"

For Lils,
in memory of those long-ago days
of "the Es and the As"
A. J. P.

To my kids, Haven and Liam
A. R.

ISBN 978-0-545-78453-5

Text copyright © 2013 by Ammi-Joan Paquette.
Illustrations copyright © 2013 by Adam Record.
All rights reserved. Published by Scholastic Inc.,
557 Broadway, New York, NY 10012, by arrangement with
Candlewick Press. SCHOLASTIC and associated logos are
trademarks and/or registered trademarks of Scholastic Inc.

12 11 10 9 8 7 6 5 4 3 2   16 17 18 19/0

Printed in the U.S.A.   40

First Scholastic printing, October 2014

This book was typeset in Historical Fell Type Roman and Garrotflower.
The illustrations were created digitally.